Praise for
Tiny Vessels

"To read these seventeen gem-like dispatches from a dreamlike world is to receive a lovely condensed version of what life on earth is like, and to be blessed with a feeling full of fondness and of longing for a kinder, more natural world."

George Saunders, Booker Prize-winning author of
Lincoln in the Bardo and *Tenth of December*

"JR Fenn's vessels are Fabergé eggs, mermaid's purses, and light-filled hulls. Each offers a window into a world both strange and familiar. Together they become an airship that moves from the heartbreakingly intimate to the startling and expansive. Fenn's stories are precise and wise, restrained and delightful, tiny but never small. An absolutely exquisite debut."

Sonja Livingston, author of *Ghostbread*

"The vessels may be tiny, but the worlds contained in this collection are immense. These small stories ache and breathe and sing and dream, contemplating everything from the inside of the tiniest seed to the farthest reaches of the universe. With taut, poetic prose, Fenn's work captures the complexity and wonder of existing."

Tara Campbell, author of *City of Dancing Gargoyles*
and *Midnight at the Organporium*

"These stories are lush in both their everydayness and their strangeness. Even those rooted in the ordinary world read like dispatches from somewhere else, because JR Fenn has a way of cracking open what you didn't know could open. *Tiny Vessels* is a surprising and captivating collection—a dreamy delight from a writer I'll eagerly follow into any world she unearths."

Michelle N. Ross, author of *They Kept Running*

"For those of us who worship at the altar of literature *Tiny Vessels* is a new star in the firmament, every sentence a benediction, startling in its narrative precision, its lyrical grace, the primacy of its storytelling. From the earliest sentences of *Tiny Vessels* it's clear we are in the hands of an anointed master, a visionary stylist, a practitioner of ancient word magics and timeless mythologies, wielding the word as prayer and testimony, a passionate interrogation of the human condition, each faceted compaction of narrative essentialism touching the reader with awe and wonderment. Every once in a while, a work, a writer, comes along to remind us, literature is grace, God is good."

Arthur Flowers, author of *Another Good Loving Blues* and *De Mojo Blues*

Tiny
Vessels

JR Fenn

RED MARE
PRESS

TINY VESSELS

Published in partnership with *The Masters Review*, an online literary journal.

www.mastersreview.com / contact@mastersreview.com

Edited by Cole Meyer.

Cover design by Emelie Mano.

Interior design by Julianne Johnson.

Red Mare Press / Discover New Art, LLC

70 SW Century Drive, Suite 100442, Bend, Oregon 97702

www.redmarepress.com

Red Mare Press is a division of Discover New Art, LLC.

The Red Mare Press name and logo are trademarks of Discover New Art, LLC.

The publisher is not responsible for websites (or their content) that are not owned by the publisher.

ISBN 9798990183896

Printed in the United States of America.

To June and Rosie
for showing me the greatest things
come in the smallest packages

CONTENTS

INTRODUCTION

by Rita Bullwinkel

THESE SEVENTEEN STORIES circle the potent, high-centrate questions of life. What parts of our childhood selves live in our adult bodies? If humans left Earth, would they lose their humanity? What is the nature of emotional inheritance? How are the stories we tell road maps for how we might walk through life? Is narrative a vessel? If so, what's inside? Can what's inside a life be both immense and small at the same time?

The delights in these pages are manifold and maximalist. In some stories we're in a post-earth, space-station-inhabiting human civilization where the memory of dogs is so distant that it might be a fiction. In other stories we're inside the primordial soup where humans have yet to exist. These stories swerve wildly from the familiar world, to the invented, to the uncanny, while always inhabiting the texture of a true emotional reality.

Cherry trees blossom. Mothers die and leave heirlooms for their daughters. Match boxes from childhood are treasured. Interstates change. Apple Danishes are eaten. Stories are told and then forgotten.

The rhythm of this collection feels like whitewater rafting. The swerves are radical, and unexpected. These stories splash, shock, and subvert expectations. JR Fenn is a master of collage and compression. She captures very large narratives within the span of just a few scenes. Her linguistic brushstrokes are broad, yet specific, intuitive, and beguiling, and communicative. Some stories read like fables, while others read like a diary. *Tiny Vessels* is a tremendous achievement. It's a book that now lives inside me.

RITA BULLWINKEL is the author of *Headshot* and *Belly Up*, a story collection that won the Believer Book Award. She is a 2022 recipient of a Whiting Award, the editor of *McSweeney's Quarterly*, a contributing editor at *NOON*, and the Picador Guest Professor of Literature at Leipzig University in Germany, where she teaches courses on creative writing, zines, and the uses of invented and foreign languages as tools for world building.

MEMORY BOX

ALL DAY LONG, THE CHILDREN are left to their own devices. They deepen the pits they're digging, line sticks along the edges to form palisades, pile gravel in the outfields to make cairns like the ones they've seen on Mars. It's a cold week, the atmosphere thin, but like children everywhere, they refuse to acknowledge that sweaters exist. The sky darkens to burnt umber. From their father's workshop comes the whir of the drill, then silence, then a stream of profanities, too muttered to make out.

What's he preparing this time? It's become a weekly ritual. *These will be memories to hold onto*, their father says. *Memories are worth their weight in gold. Do you understand?*

The children always nod, but they glance away from his tight mouth and reddened eyes, embarrassed by his fierce, tender hold on the coping saw. *Gold* is just a word in the history lessons, like *T-Rex* and *Dodo* and *Earth*.

"It's time," he calls. In the workshop, the table is clear except for a house rising from its middle. The house has windows and a sloping roof.

It's surrounded by fences. Within these fences, animals cluster. The children gawk. "It's a farm," the father says.

The farm looks nothing like the ones they've seen on the spaceships or here on their home world, where gravity outside the dome drags anything with mass too strongly toward the planet's core—the farms here are rows of square plots under artificial lights, uniform shoots struggling upward in a balding pelt, the mountains a dry smudge in the distance.

The youngest child picks up a small, four-legged creature. "That's a dog," the father says. The child emits a slight noise and cups the dog to his chest. He's always wanted a dog. He's read about them in books. A dog would lick his face, squirm in his lap. A dog would take away his loneliness. The middle child bends to peer into the kitchen.

"The sink works," the father says. "Go on, turn the faucet."

As a thin gush of water splashes into the basin, the oldest child hangs back. The garden stretches behind the house. The tiny round tomatoes still smell of primer, fresh painted in a red so bright she can almost taste it. *It's the flesh of gods,* her mother had said once. *Like ambrosia, with a twist of skunk.* She'd bunched her fingers to her lips, released them into the air.

She'd always been doing things like that—little gestures from the old world, as if she'd stepped out of one of the educational movie clips where the people's skin glowed in black and white, their celluloid faces relaxed, never imagining exodus might be likely, or possible.

There'd come the day when her mother had grasped at her hand, too weak in those last hours to exert much force. *Everyone on this mudball's just trying to do their best,* she'd said.

Out there, her body floats in space, sheathed in its pod after the sky burial ceremony.

The hovercraft driver had lost his license, but that doesn't matter. *Some people are reckless,* the oldest child thinks. *And should never be forgiven.* But then, against her bitterness, she can hear her mother's voice, song-like. She can see her—sighing, looking out at the new galaxy, turning to speak, her eyes glistening. *Starwalkers,* she murmurs. *We're starseeds, spangled through the universe, so far from home. We're transplants, taking root.*

"Here," the father says. He's holding out a tiny basket, woven of dead grass.

The oldest child doesn't ask where he got the grass, or the water. Her thumb and forefinger forage, clumsy and huge, in the tomato plants. Soon the basket is full. The youngest child is whispering to the toy in his hands. The middle child is holding her knuckle before her eyes as a tear of water gathers itself, readying to drop. The father's rearranging the graveyard, shuffling two headstones closer in the fake peat. And the oldest child's hearing rain rattling down, or what she's imagined rain would sound like—it's pattering onto her toes, dry pebbles of raintorrent pinging against the floor, the tomatoes sliding from their basket, askew in her hand, and the sound is just as if it were pouring so hard the garden soil is drenched through, and she's in a dark kitchen, her mother canning at the stove, the soft tomatoes brined and sealed, a dog barking to be let in.

Wind Horse

For a long time, I lived in my childhood—first as a child, then for many years after. I sat on the back patio and spit watermelon seeds into the grass where the snakes soaked up the sun. My mother made pies with rhubarb from the garden, the stalks softening as they baked in cups of sugar, the crust hot and sweet. My father mowed the lawn, whirling across the ground until the yellowjackets belched from below in thick black clouds. At night, peepers sang in the puddles. Panthers traveled along secret corridors up and down the mountain. At the bottom of the hill below the driveway, crawfish lurked in the creek. Once I found a baby mole near the lilies of the valley by the mailboxes, its mother nowhere to be seen. I held it in my palm, its tiny paws pink and grasping. A plastic cup with dirt and grass at the bottom made a terrarium. I dropped in bits of food that went uneaten, tipped water from a bottlecap into the well of its mouth, dug a grave in the lilies of the valley when its little form went stiff. I remember driving through the farm near my house, the weathervane on the farmhouse roof a brass horse rearing toward the future, the stream by the cornfield that engulfed the road during heavy rains. I remember the black dog that rushed from the dark at the side of the road as I rounded a bend. My car slid on the pavement, spun. When it stopped I was looking back in the direction I'd been coming from. I was empty and light as those days on the hilltop across from my house, my chest lifting toward the mountains and the sky beyond, mouth open to drink the wind.

THE CHERRY TREE

WE MOVED TO A SMALL CITY by the Great Lakes from another country. The cherry tree in the front yard bloomed not long after we moved in. That winter, a storm split the trunk.

It has to come down, the tree guy said. And then as he turned to leave: So, where are you all from?

I'd picked up an accent from my years of living in the country of my husband's birth. I pretended to hear my daughter inside.

A few weeks later, the truck pulled up. The door opened. A silver crutch stuck out.

A tree fell on me, he said. Shattered my leg.

Are you sure you want to go ahead?

The crew cut off the branches, sectioned the base. A bulldozer dug out the roots and carried them across the sky in torn-apart chunks.

What about the hole? I said. It gaped, a crater between the house and the street.

What about it?

You said you'd fill it in.

After they'd gone, I found the contract in a pile of papers. *When we remove the beautiful tree from your yard, we pledge to fill up the hole, smooth it over, seed grass, leave it as if the tree never was.*

I called the tree company. They sent a crew to fill in the hole.

A truck began driving past the house.

The telephone rang. Hello? my husband said.

Go back where you came from, the voice said.

Late at night, there was a knock. We hid in the dark. A rain of pebbles exploded against the house's face. A truck started up, puttered off. After that, we didn't see the truck again. Grass grew over the spot where the tree had been, as though it had never been there to bloom, or be ruined, or taken away.

HEDGIES

Mᴄʏ ᴄʜɪʟᴅʀᴇɴ ᴡɪsʜ ᴛᴏ ᴋɴᴏᴡ about the following things: wind, darkness, and hedgehogs. They each have a small stuffed hedgehog. They have aptly named their stuffed hedgehogs Hedgie. They cover cardboard boxes in green construction paper, cut windows and doors, glue jewels on balconied roofs, add their own inventions: hammocks of twine, high shelves for naps. A red pocket flashlight stuck through the roof provides ample light. At night, when the wind blows, the Hedgies are safe, the windows of their houses dark with sleep. What do the Hedgies dream in their beds? Outside, long shadows under forests of grass.

After the Natatorium

The first time they saw the natatorium they changed into their bathing costumes, pulled their rubber caps over their heads, and rushed into the water without a thought for the ice crystals that floated, cold and perfect, on the surface. As they somersaulted, chicken-fought, and cannonballed from the edges, an Indiana marching band played the young upstart Sousa's "The Liberty Bell," conducted by a gesticulating barber from Mishawaka. The pool washed their skin clean of Chicago grime—soot from the chimneys, brick dust from fingernails, mortar packed and matted in their hair—and they crawled out of the natatorium as pink and fat as they had from the baptismal font, before they could rightly remember their own names.

At night the natatorium's locked doors and windows invited the jimmied entrance of gin-breathers and wounded boys who immersed themselves in the waters, where they bled through their bandages in a hush, leaving the pool's liquid a clear lapping blue and their wounds salted, closed, and covered over with quick growths of scar tissue that shone

9

whiter against the white bottom of the great basin—a basin so gigantic that none of the night gangs could have imagined it could hold them all together at once as they bobbed and spumed and sighed in the dark, the occasional laugh that bubbled up from their throats swallowed by the cavernous heights above.

As the water warmed over the course of the summer, swimmers arrived from all corners of the city: babies with cauls that clung wet in their mothers' arms, dancers whose jewels spread from their hips in drifts of color, liberated minnows that darted in bright curtains though the depths, a dromedary with levers inside to propel its dives toward the bottom-most deeps where it dwindled smaller than the terriers that paddled belly down in the light-cracked shallows.

Soon the demand for water outpaced the supply from the spring-fed aqueducts sourced in a village northwest of the city. The natatorium dried up into a hollow field of concrete that first housed an electrical exhibit, then a market, and then—before it finally fell into disrepair—a variety show. Hawkers lingered by the entrance to advertise big mamas, one-eyed dogs and penguin men, flippers downed in black and white fuzz. The waterless pool filled with a honeycomb of curtained compartments where hundreds of people disappeared, eyes open in wonder, in hopes that others might chart their futures.

Always

IT WAS A THREE-WAY INTERSECTION without a walk sign. The snow pelted sideways. I found what I needed at the back. A customer perused the beer, his balance precarious. The cashier scanned, stopped—it was cash or debit only. "I'll put them back," I said. "No!" The customer sailed up the aisle, toting a twelve-pack. "You *need* that." He was covered with construction site dust. "She *needs* that," he said to the cashier, gallantly. They shooed me out. Through the glass, I saw the cashier add to the sale, the crumpled bills held out by the guy like a gas-station bouquet.

Fumigation Day

I OPEN THE CEDAR CHEST and shake out the first thing that comes to hand. My green sweater, weave intact, no holes.

It's a good cedar chest, an old one.

I'm going to give it to Chloe.

I'm giving all of my wool sweaters to Goodwill. In Florida, I'm wearing cotton T-shirts and cotton shorts that show my knees. I never liked pools but I'm going to lie by the pool in that little community I found online and stick my chest up toward the sun while I smoke and get leathery.

The doorbell rings. Through the eyehole I see the fumigation guy, his nose huge and the rest of his face receding. He bobs forward and back as if he were admiring himself in the bottom of an upside-down stainless-steel bowl.

His nametag says Ken. I let him in and he unzips a yellow nylon bag, takes out a white nylon suit, steps into it. Ken disappears and an astronaut takes his place. He bends down to inspect my carpet, gets down on hands and knees and looks for eggs in the threads through his face mask.

Maybe Chloe won't want the cedar chest. Maybe her apartment is too small for family heirlooms. Maybe she doesn't wear wool anymore. Last time I saw her she kissed me on the cheek and a smell washed over me like lilies of the valley. She never wore perfume. Her hair glittered in the sun and she smiled a kind of smile I didn't recognize.

I knew all her smiles when she was a baby—the smile that said she thought my jokes were kind of funny, the one that said she wanted a strawberry real bad, the one that said she had to quench a thirst so deep it made her flap her arms and hold them out toward me to nurse, a half-smile of pure need, pure certainty.

She said, "Why Florida, Mom?" as she smiled this smile I didn't understand.

I wave my hands at Ken and go upstairs to the bedroom with the walk-in closet. His boots thunk behind me, his breath wheezes through his suit vent.

I open the door of the closet and duck as a cloud of white moths pours out over my head.

Ken moves forward and stands at the door, his arms spread, his gloved hands touching the doorjambs. As I back away, I see Ken's man-shaped suit silhouetted in a pale kaleidoscope of moths that stream up, down, and around in the closet.

The boards feel cool and solid underneath me. The light hits the water as I dangle my feet off the dock. A blackfly lands in my hair. As I comb it out, it buzzes in my fingers. My sweater smells sharp, medicinal, fresh.

In Florida, the fumigators wrap whole houses in plastic and pipe the poison in through a nozzle. You can't go back in for two weeks.

My house looks like the outside of a house, with shingles and windows and a roof. Not at all like a giant plastic bag.

I don't look back at it, though. I know what it looks like.

Ken bobs through the rooms like a helium balloon, dropping poison.

The rocks crop up as the tide goes out. The seagulls hunker down on the stone outcroppings and send mean, defiant shrugs to no one in particular.

Chloe can have whatever she wants but she can't fit that much in her apartment. New York apartments are really small. There's not that much room for stuff. The antique furniture my father made—the Shaker tables, the bookshelves, the spice rack.

The high chair where she met her first blackberry. Blackberry juice all over her hands, up her bare arms, smeared in a purple stain across her cheeks, her little knob of a chin. Blackberries on the floor, splatted on the white wall behind the high chair, smashed all over the high chair's tray, juice dripping down its legs.

I swing my feet. A wind comes up and cuts through my green sweater. I shiver.

A fog of poison lingers in the house. Ken can't work the window latches in his foil gloves, but he leaves them on, fumbling around without accomplishing anything.

I go through the house and open all the windows to the cold.

In the kitchen, which soon feels arctic, I offer Ken a glass of water.

He takes off his helmet. His hands crackle as he drinks.

Ken looks at the pictures on my refrigerator.

Ken has a baby. Her name is Claire, seven months. He curls his spaceman arms to his chest as though he can't stand her absence, as though she might be right there in his fumigation hug.

We stroll through the house. The dead moths puff out under our feet.

We wind up in the attic. The light from the dormer cuts through the dust and the poison smog in a thick ray. All the furniture looms in heaps.

I brush a pile of moths off the high chair tray, off the chair back with its hand-carved leaves and roses.

I pick it up, so brittle and tiny.

I shove it at Ken. I insist that he take it. I don't need it anymore, don't want it.

He refuses.

I carry it down the attic stairs and outside, set it down by the tailgate of his white fumigation truck.

The peg legs sink into the spring mud.

We argue. He gives in and puts the high chair in the back of his truck, where it rattles as he drives away, skittering across the truck bed like a live thing as he disappears around the bend.

After the sound of the truck dies out, I walk down the drive to the mailbox. I pull my sweater tight around me as the evening chill sets in and the smell of the sap cuts through the air. When I get back to the house, it's dark.

THE MATCHBOX

WHEN I WAS A CHILD I loved a little matchbox. It was made of cardboard, long and thin, small enough to disappear in a child's palm. I carried it everywhere I went. I loved everything about this matchbox. Its lightness, the way it grew damp in my grasp. The way the drawer slid open to reveal a tiny holding place. It has sometimes been said that the longing for small things is a longing for life. But what is the longing for a holding place too small to hold much of anything? This is something I wonder all the time.

THE INTERSTATE

THESE DAYS I DRIVE THE I-390 past trees just splotched with red. For three years I lived in a country without autumn, where nothing ever died, and now even the grasses in the verge turn yellow, tall stalks proud that they're on their way out. I'm on my way out, too. as I travel down the slow road.

Sixty-five gets the best gas mileage, sometimes sixty, and everyone passes me as the sun makes the car a transparent bowl that carries me past long fields razed with wheat, hot and golden-armed. These fields have turned to graveyards, a young man this morning caught in the jaws of a baler. I can see the bow of his mother's back as she bends over his head. I'm dying a different kind of death, the death that happens when youth rushes into your body, far into its silent center, where you feel it quicken in cell divisions, but it's not yours.

Every day, the clouds roll off to the edge of the fields and disappear. The sky opens into a clear basket of sun upended over these farms and woods, so bright I squint to see the road. I began to die the day my firstborn stared

17

with weird, blind love at the patterns of light that crackled across her eyes the way a pool's surface throws shadows over its white floor. She looked past me to the place where she'd come from, a place that looked like the koi pond I leaned over one summer as a teenager, the water tangled with vines where fish glided too far down to see as anything but slow movements illuminated from below. I loved a boy then, his hair a lion's ruff around his head, his movements so quick he disappeared into the trees.

Some parts of us die before the others. The wind whips the car with the force of a comet's tail. The gust flattens the fields, dust dashes against the windshield, glitters up and away. It sends shivers through my spine, my body bent on a point inside that expands faster than fireflies loosed through the mouth of a glass bottle. I have seen my firstborn run away, laughing. Part of me will stretch outside myself, spreading with my daughters over places I'll never see. Part of me will stay here, tired and small, as the world dies around me in fresh, clear breaths.

POSTCARD FROM INFINITY

I WAS GIVEN THE CHANCE for a holiday, so I took it. *Come rest,* the advertisement squawked through the drone's speaker on a rainy day. *Take the rest you deserve in the offworld landscape of your choice.* I'd been working hard for a very long time. Given the options of desert, spaceship, or seaside, I chose them all. *Are you sure?* the agent wrote. *Yes,* I replied. *Without a doubt. It's precisely what I need to rest and recharge.*

First, I went to the desert. Rock spires towered above dry riverbeds. I swept between ground and sky in an old-fashioned wooden ship with sails. At the café on a ledge halfway up the canyon wall, I asked for water. *We don't have that here,* the proprietor said, his face shadowed by his newsboy cap. *What do you have?* I asked. *Nothing and everything,* he answered. *Oh, excellent,* I said. *I'll take that.*

In the spaceship I wandered through a biodome of plants. I came across a shovel beside what seemed to be a grave. A robot stood, rusted, under a giant fern. Raindrops fell from the glass above, plastering my hair to my head. Somewhere a bird called. The noise reminded me of my name, which I couldn't place. In the bushes, berries weighted the branches, so loaded they drooped. I tried to pick some, but my hands didn't work. On all fours, I ate the fruit. *Sunshine,* I thought, as the juices dribbled from my mouth. *They taste of sun, where the sun is not.*

At the seaside, I floated above a long beach. Gulls glided over white-caps on cerulean waves. I stood in the middle of a disc under a semicircle of glass, the movements of the hovercraft so smooth I didn't need to hold the tiller. My hands at my sides were shortening, flattening, soldering together like a fish's fins. An image from a distant moment of my life—some time to come, or having passed—flashed through my mind: two daughters chasing birds, gathering eggs from the ground. They held the eggs in their hands. *Breakfast,* they called. The gold of the yolk shone through the shell. Creatures crawled up from the shallows onto the shining sand, and I was one of them, too, all of us crawling toward our future along that illuminated shore.

*T*RANSFER

THE SMELL OF COLOGNE comes on a burst of wind as the sun beats down and the gulls wing past overhead. I breathed this smell as a teenager in a pedestrian lane like this one: there had been a busker then, a cellist with a red velvet case that yawned wide and a hot pastry with apple soon after. The rays of the sun stream round me and my younger self rises up in a rush. The windows of the shops gleam with clear views onto chrome espresso machines and white-painted furniture as the glass reflects passersby. I slide along with the others and a long room looms inwards with figures at tables. Someone leans forward behind the glass, an arm's length away. I lean in and a face rushes up to meet me, the burnt smell of coffee, the din of people talking. I sink back into myself and stir my coffee with a spoon; foam clings to the silver below the back of my hand, freckled brown and soft. Walkers move by in the background, quiet in the sun. The light shoots through the window. Someone looks in at me through the glass, hair ablaze in the halo of the afternoon. I bite into my apple Danish.

Central Schools Resolution
No. 2153

CLOWN SIGHTINGS HAD GOTTEN out of hand, the school board determined at the most contentious meeting in recent history. The clowns had started in the woods, a bob of orange hair slipping away into the brush, a puff-suited figure on a farm horizon. Everyone thought it was a joke, something to do with the upcoming elections. Some people thought it meant something—a comment on media saturation or the voting public's sense of being stuck at a clown show; others contended it was only meant to seem to mean something in order to reveal the absurdity of assigning meaning through the attribution of intentionality in the first place. I mean, they're clowns, people said. You can't take them seriously.

Then came reports from streets at the edge of town, convenience store aisles, the gazebo in the middle of the town square, where a small child gazed up into the raccoon eyes of a clown whose white face broke apart as he smiled to show his yellow teeth. Clowns climbed into cars people left unlocked in their driveways and wandered through back doors propped open for air, greasy fingerprints smeared on refrigerator handles. People found their beds disturbed, a curly red hair shed in a clean sea of sheets. Bathroom toiletries became disarranged, a powder puff replaced in the cold cream jar. The clowns never took anything, never hurt anyone. They drifted through the ritual spaces of suburban twilight, standing outside bedroom windows as parents did story time and tucked their small charges tight under the covers. They sat on backyard swings in the dark, still as wax statues, gone by morning as if they had never been there at all.

The meeting progressed through its standard agenda and then opened to other business, which devolved into a variety of opinions about clowns shouted from every corner. When the board regained control, some members of the audience had climbed onto desks and one beefy father balanced on the windowsill, fist pumping as he underlined the importance of *protecting our children*. The president of the board spoke in a reassuring tone, her face marvelously controlled as phrases that appeared to her to be utter nonsense flowed from her lips—promises to *find a resolution to the so-called clown conspiracy* and *mount a long-term clown response strategy that cannot fail given our community's wholehearted commitment to what is clearly an issue of utmost importance*. No one could remember who proposed the idea, but once aired it caught on like wildfire, and as soon as the motion was made and seconded, a swift vote brought it to a close, as everyone present could see the merit in the resolution as well as its obvious expediency given upcoming school events.

Circulated by email and posted on the announcements board, Central Schools Resolution No. 2153 read: *Due to local, state, and national concerns with clowns and clown stories, clown costumes will NOT be allowed in school this year.*

With the arrival of the day appointed for costume wearing, however, the proclamation had some unanticipated effects. There were your usual witches and goblins and ghosts and the occasional art supply or frozen dessert maneuvering around blindly on stubby child legs. But roving in bands on the track, in the parking lot, on the sidewalks that led to the school, in the school basement, auditorium, gym, and through honeycombs of classrooms—were tons and tons of clowns. The district's consolidation into one campus meant they came in all sizes: two-foot clowns lugging backpacks half their weight by straps that threatened to break and six-foot clowns with wigs so tall their hair leaned like the crenelated hill of a soft serve about to slip off its cone. Their faces painted in reds and blues, purples and grays, stripes and dots and seven-hued rainbows, their clown suits tasseled and glittered and checked, their clown shoes several sizes too big galumphing through linoleum hallways, merry whorls of clowns slipped into their seats and back out again, disguised by their finery and their guerrilla tactics of switching places with one another so all attempts at roll call failed and the school day dissolved into pointless announcements about the passage of resolution whatever whatever and appropriate costuming and natural consequences for those who ignored the agreed-upon edict. But no one could agree on how to punish the clowns—a clown-filled detention defied imagination (and missed the point, as some hastened to add)—and that night the gaudies slipped out of their clown suits into normal pajama getups, their cheeks tinged with hints of pink and green, their hair matted close with the sweat of the show, their faces still smiling with the remnants of painted grins as they slept. They dreamed of their compadres roaming quiet streets, all the house windows darkened, the flicker of streetlights illuminating the electric frizz of hair as waddling backs moved off into the night, a silent shuffle on to the next town, a Midwest ripe for the taking.

OUR ANCESTORS DREAMED, TOO, IN THE PRIMORDIAL SOUP

A CHIMPANZEE SIGNS *coffee* in her sleep. Elephants dream every three or four days. A dolphin's left eye stays open while her right hemisphere slumbers. An octopus flails its arms, turns red, inks. Cats claw the air, chase balls of yarn, arch their backs. An eel opens and closes her mouth, her head hanging toward the riverbed. She snores, suspended in the deep. A somnolent budgie squawks, *Hey whatcha doing baby*. A finch's voice box moves in silence. A dozing bee twitches its proboscis, gathering pollen. Even seeds dream—the memory of winter tells them when to grow, when to blossom.

Green Walls Lit in the Night

At the point when part of me knew our relationship would be over soon, we were living in a country governed by its military. We lived on the top floor of a hotel. Our room had been built on the roof and was surrounded by roof on three sides, becalmed in tiles.

There were rolling brownouts in this city. When the restaurant lights went out, the staff heated the bottoms of candles and fixed them to the backs of empty chairs. The cook moved in the dark to the glow of embers and the waiters would suddenly appear in brilliant white shirtfronts, stepping into the ring of candlelight around our table.

In this city trucks thundered by on the street carrying teak logs. The trucks were so heavy their wheels cracked the pavement. The appetite for teak could not be satisfied by the last of the teak forests being harvested up north. The city contained many old buildings that had been made of teak when it was plentiful. So people dismantled the buildings and shipped their walls and floorboards abroad.

Night after night I sat on the roof as inside he watched news of the war.

The air was damp and hot, a treetop of glossy leaves near where I stationed my chair beginning to flower. Here and there, from under the door at my back, the muffled strains of the BBC World Service theme song broke the silence of curfew, the road deserted. We each observed what we could. For him, it was drone strikes, casualties, changes in market shares. As for me, I needed to be outside. I watched as the house across the street was taken apart. I never saw anyone working on the house, only the steps of its dissolution. The lights hung around the insides of the house bathed what remained of its structure—just floor supports and center joists, by the time I left—in an end-of-days glow, as if this were the kind of house where we'd all find ourselves at one time or another, near the vanishing point of our lives.

Later I learned about a river monster who pulls people into the water. If you meet one, bow. The creature will bow back, spilling the water from the bowl it carries on its head, and it will return to the river for more. I could never forget this bowing and emptying, these bowls filling and emptying again, in an endless sequence of absence and possibility. A space will always be filled by something, even if it's not what you expect.

ALTOGETHER

I WAS BORN A MOTHER of three children on an island in the north. Every day I put one on my back and two in their stroller and went out to the coffee shop. I felt our bodies move forward; we lifted our faces and breathed cold air as the wheels turned under our weight. She was beautiful and stoic in her white hat with her babies all around her. We never mentioned that we watched her through the window glass, the absence in her wake; a silence grew and then our eyes drifted back to our books. No one had known her in that country as a child; no one knew her history, her parentage; had watched her skin her knees, be gathered by friends in packs, grow wiser with age. One day she emerged, taller than anyone had imagined, from her whitewashed house with blue shutters, her babies in her arms. They were all small then, light enough to carry at once, their mitted feet dangling loose by her thighs. "You never learned to be all right," he said, "to see the separations between yourself and others." Like me, he meant, as he had experienced her contiguity, her children she never let out of her sight, him who she followed and touched too until he needed to be just himself. Every day, the sun sent its first light over her doorstep, the door opened, the stroller appeared, children nestled in bright blankets, the handlebar gripped in her hands, the straps of the backpack crossed over her chest, the baby's head crowned above hers, the blue door closed and locked with her gold key, along the shell path and onto the sidewalk, past one, two, three houses to the corner, past the hat shop, the cycle shop, the B&B, the new book shop, the used book shop, the outdoor clothing shop, the art shop, and now the fur shop, waiting to cross the street altogether. We admire the whole arrangement. The whites and blacks and grays go by in shapes and we come near and then closer and then we are there.

TAPESTRY

OUR MOTHERS WERE ARTISTS, and after they passed we cherished
their art. We put their paintings on our walls, their jewelry on our necks,
their blankets on the back of our couches or at the foot of our beds. Some
of us continued their work, in our studios suffused with light, jars of tur-
pentine on acrylic-splashed tabletops where we labored over portraits or
still lives or abstracts with our brushes. Many of our grandchildren found
themselves drawn to local art classes, pinching pots or throwing bowls on
the wheel, or making pale sparks cascade from the soldering iron onto the
floor. When the floods arrived, the children of our grandchildren planted
gardens underwater—labyrinths of kelp rippling, lit with solar rays, sea-
flowers plaited into crowns and salt fronds gathered at the harvest. Above
the sea, inland from the coasts, where the land had parched to desert, our
descendants wove baskets to hang from trees, swinging their children to
sleep above the raking winds. And then the cataclysm, the exodus. Lifted
into the vacuum, those children scattered, landed in their pods, turned
to look back at the tiny blue marble, breathing, which had once been

their home. They built domes of air and light. Our lineage terraformed the dark side of the moon into fruit-bearing orchards. Those carrying our mothers' spirits dyed cloth with vermilion husks, wove it with starstuff, and dwelled forever in tents of beauty.

MESSAGE IN A BOTTLE

WE SAT AROUND THE FIRE singing John Prine. *Don't hide your candle under a bushel,* my mother always said, but I did, my mouth shut tight—the mouth, angelic in its sounds, that if opened would sing down the stars. *Well, if you want to get rich…* an acquaintance later said, on the other side of the Atlantic after I'd somehow played and sung. But I couldn't imagine such a thing. Around the fire, the Pleiades glistening above like spit in an oyster's maw, sparks hissed and stung our skin, where the smell of chipotles and sour cream lingered; you clop-clopped your hand against the guitar, and a traveler from far away shook his head to the beat, handsome and reeking of his tent, and your fellow smokejumper— craggy faced in the dark—hummed off key, and our neighbor from the next trailer over plucked her mandolin. You crooned so gently about our small panic attacks at adversity, and I wanted to complement the notes but didn't, as if I'd forgotten wailing along with Fleetwood Mac the fall I'd learned to drive, rip-roaring beyond the speed limit and belting at full volume, catapulting through the fresh mountain air and shouting within,

Listen to me, I love the world, and I'm dying too. So why do I send words out in my absence? If they're found and read, they make a harmony now.

ACKNOWLEDGEMENTS

With deepest thanks to my parents, Scott and Barbara, for showing me how to live a creative life. To my husband, Lytton, for sharing a life of words. To June and Rosie, for inspiring me always. To Misty, Toothless, Stoick, Gobber, Lily, and Meggie, for bringing our household such joy. To TBK, and my Library writing group, for so much moral support and excellent advice along the way. To SWENJ, for helping many of these pieces arrive at their current form. To the editors who selected some of these stories for publication—Lynn Mundell, Megan M. Garr, James Thomas, Michelle Ross and F.E. Choe, Sonja Livingston, Hattie Fletcher, Ian Chung, Mark D. Anderson, Paula Read, and Roxane Gay—for their votes of confidence in the work. To the judges of the Annual Writing By Writers' Short Short Writing Contest, the Bristol Short Story Prize, and the New Millennium Award for Flash Fiction, for their encouragement. To my mentors, friends, and colleagues at Syracuse University and SUNY College of Environmental Science and Forestry, for expanding my love and understanding of the writing life. To Cole Meyer and the whole team at *The Masters Review*, for being a pleasure to work with. And of course to Rita Bullwinkel, for choosing *Tiny Vessels*, and for making it possible for me to hold a book I wrote in my hands for the first time.

"Memory Box" appeared in the *Bristol Short Story Prize Anthology Volume 17,* and was awarded the 59th Annual New Millenium Award for Flash Fiction.

"Wind Horse" appeared in *Centaur* (Winter 2025).

"The Cherry Tree" appeared in the *Bath Flash Fiction Anthology 2024.*

"After the Natatorium" appeared in *Versal 11.*

"Fumigation Day" appeared in *SmokeLong Quarterly.*

"The Matchbox" appeared in *100 Word Story.*

"The Interstate" appeared in *Stone Canoe 10,* and was reprinted in *Short Reads.*

"Transfer" appeared in *Eunoia Review.*

"Central Schools Resolution No. 2153" appeared in *Flash Fiction Magazine.*

"Green Walls Lit in the Night" appeared in *Panorama: The Journal of Travel, Place, and Nature,* in the *Cities* issue.

"Altogether" appeared in *PANK.*

"Message in a Bottle" won the 11th Annual Writing By Writers' Short Short Writing Contest.

JR FENN writes about the living web of the human and more-than-human world as it changes over time. Her work has appeared in many places, including *Boston Review*, *DIAGRAM*, *Split Lip*, *PANK, 100 Word Story*, the Bath Flash Fiction Anthology, and the Bristol Short Story Prize Anthology. She is a graduate of the MFA program at Syracuse University, where she was awarded the Joyce Carol Oates Prize in Fiction. Other recognitions include the *Gulf Coast* Prize for Nonfiction, the 59th Annual New Millennium Award for Flash Fiction, and *Stone Canoe*'s Robert Colley Prize for Fiction. Her work has been supported by the Key West Literary Seminar, the *Orion* Environmental Writers' Workshop, Writing by Writers, The Writers' Colony at Dairy Hollow, and Hewnoaks, among other places. She teaches Fiction and Environmental Writing at State University of New York College of Environmental Science and Forestry and lives in Western New York with her family.